The Elephant
and the Bad Baby

Story by ELFRIDA VIPONT
Illustrations by RAYMOND BRIGGS

SCHOLASTIC BOOK SERVICES
NEW YORK • TORONTO • LONDON • AUCKLAND • SYDNEY • TOKYO

Copyright © 1969 by Elfrida Vipont. Copyright © 1969 by Raymond Briggs. This edition is published by Scholastic Book Services, a division of Scholastic Magazines, Inc., by arrangement with Coward, McCann & Geoghegan, Inc.

3rd printing . . . . December 1974

Printed in the U.S.A.

Once upon a time
there was an Elephant.

One day the Elephant went for a walk and met a Bad Baby.
The Elephant said to the Bad Baby, "Would you like a ride?"
The Bad Baby said yes.

So the Elephant reached out his trunk.

He picked up the Bad Baby and put him on his back.

And they went rumpeta, rumpeta, rumpeta, all down the road.

Soon they met an ice cream man.
The Elephant said to the Bad Baby, "Would you like some ice cream?"
The Bad Baby said yes.

So the Elephant reached out his trunk.
He took some ice cream for himself.
He took some ice cream for the Bad Baby.
And they went rumpeta, rumpeta, rumpeta, all down the road.

The ice cream man came running after them.

Next, they came to a butcher's shop.
The Elephant said to the Bad Baby, "Would you like a meat pie?"
The Bad Baby said yes.

So the Elephant reached out his trunk.
He took a pie for himself.
He took a pie for the Bad Baby.
And they went rumpeta, rumpeta, rumpeta, all down the road.

The ice cream man and the butcher
came running after them.

Next, they came to a baker's shop.
The Elephant said to the Bad Baby, "Would you like a bun?"
The Bad Baby said yes.

So the Elephant reached out his trunk.
He took a bun for himself.
He took a bun for the Bad Baby.
And they went rumpeta, rumpeta, rumpeta, all down the road.

The ice cream man, and the butcher, and the baker came running after them.

Next, they came to a snack shop.
The Elephant said to the Bad Baby, "Would you like some gingersnaps?"
The Bad Baby said yes.

So the Elephant reached out his trunk.
He took some gingersnaps for himself.
He took some gingersnaps for the Bad Baby.
And they went rumpeta, rumpeta, rumpeta, all down the road.

The ice cream man, and the butcher, and the baker,
and the snack shop man came running after them.

Next, they came to a grocery store.
The Elephant said to the Bad Baby, "Would you like a chocolate cookie?"
The Bad Baby said yes.

So the Elephant reached out his trunk.
He took a chocolate cookie for himself.
He took a chocolate cookie for the Bad Baby.
And they went rumpeta, rumpeta, rumpeta, all down the road.

The ice cream man, and the butcher, and the baker,
and the snack shop man, and the grocer came running after them.

Next, they came to a candy store.
The Elephant said to the Bad Baby, "Would you like a lollipop?"
The Bad Baby said yes.

So the Elephant reached out his trunk.
He took a lollipop for himself.
He took a lollipop for the Bad Baby.
And they went rumpeta, rumpeta, rumpeta, all down the road.

The ice cream man, and the butcher, and the baker, and the snack shop man,
and the grocer, and the candy-store lady came running after them.

Next, they came to a fruit and vegetable stand.
The Elephant said to the Bad Baby, "Would you like an apple?"
The Bad Baby said yes.

So the Elephant reached out his trunk.
He took an apple for himself.
He took an apple for the Bad Baby.
And they went rumpeta, rumpeta, rumpeta, all down the road.

The ice cream man, and the butcher, and the baker,
and the snack shop man, and the grocer, and the candy-store lady,
and the fruit and vegetable man came running after them.

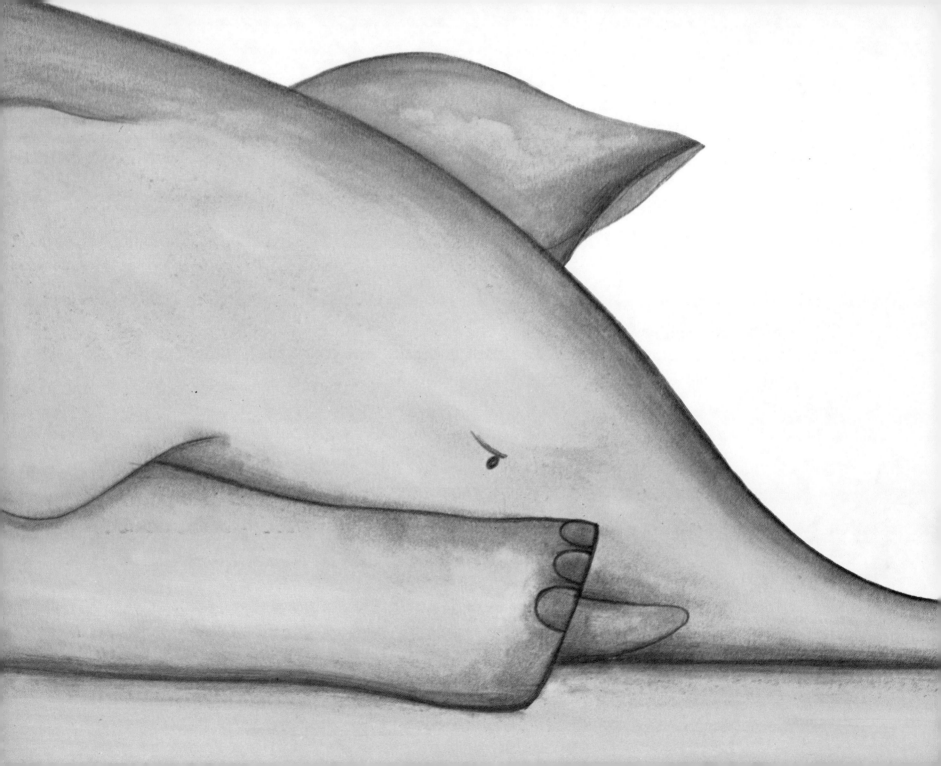

Then the Elephant said to the Bad Baby, "You haven't once said please!"
He said, "You haven't said please — not even ONCE!"
Then the Elephant sat down suddenly in the middle of the road.
The Bad Baby fell off.

And the ice cream man, and the butcher, and the baker,
and the snack shop man, and the grocer, and the candy-store lady,
and the fruit and vegetable man
all went BUMP into a heap.

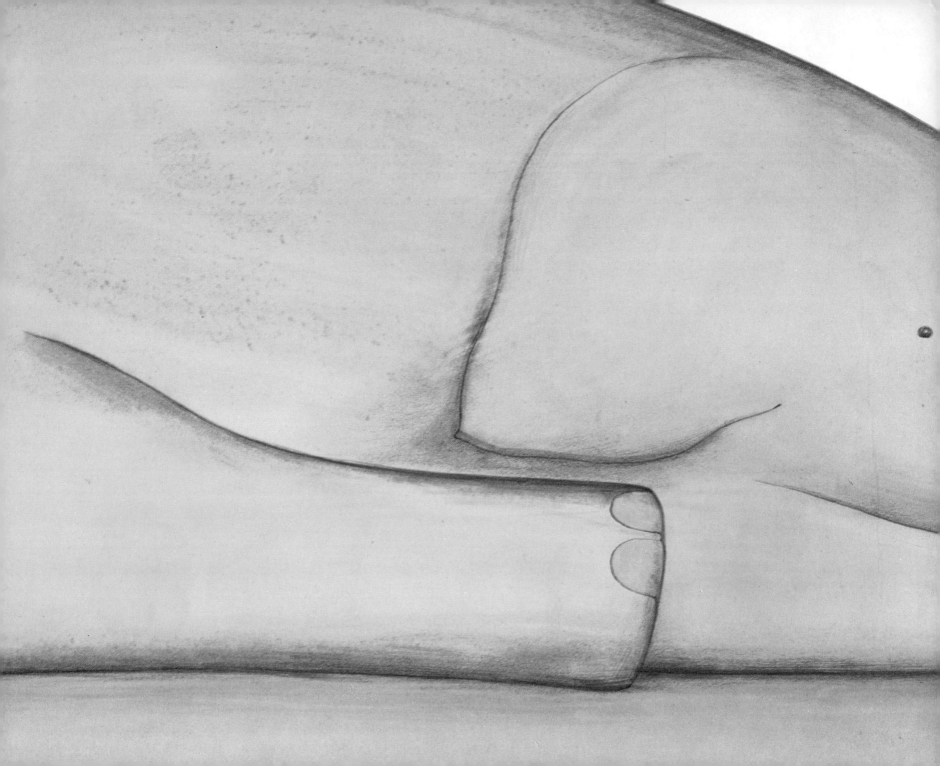

The Elephant said, "He never once said please!"

The ice cream man, and the butcher, and the baker,
and the snack shop man, and the grocer, and the candy-store lady,
and the fruit and vegetable man all got up.
They said, "Just imagine that! He never once said please!"

Then the Bad Baby said, "PLEASE! I want to go home to my mother."

So the Elephant reached out his trunk.
He picked up the Bad Baby and put him on his back.
And they went rumpeta, rumpeta, rumpeta, all down the road.

And the ice cream man, and the butcher, and the baker,
and the snack shop man, and the grocer, and the candy-store lady,
and the fruit and vegetable man
all came running after them.

The Bad Baby's mother saw them.
She said, "Have you all come for supper?"
The Bad Baby said, "Yes, PLEASE!"
So they all went in and had supper.
The Bad Baby's mother made pancakes for everybody.

Then the Elephant went rumpeta, rumpeta, rumpeta,
all down the road.
The ice cream man, and the butcher, and the baker,
and the snack shop man, and the grocer, and the candy-store lady,
and the fruit and vegetable man all went running after him.

But the Bad Baby went to bed.